HAZEL NUTT
MAD SCIENTIST
by David Elliott illustrated by True Kelley

Holiday House / New York

"Cat-Fish"
patent pending:
Hazel Nutt

To Lisa Hull,
Mad and fabulous as they come
D. E.

To my brother,
Mark Kelley, Mad Scientist
T. K.

Text copyright © 2003 by David Elliott
Illustrations copyright © 2003 by True Kelley
All Rights Reserved
Printed in the United States of America
The text typeface is Kosmik Bold One.
The illustrations are rendered in pen and ink, watercolor,
and Formula X (patent pending: Hazel Nutt).
www.holidayhouse.com
First Edition

Library of Congress Cataloging-in-Publication Data

Elliott, David, 1947–
Hazel Nutt, mad scientist / by David Elliott; illustrated by True Kelley.
p. cm.
Summary: When the mad scientist Dr. Hazel Nutt begins creating monsters again,
the angry villagers of Hamburg-with-Ketchup storm her laboratory but
are in for a pleasant surprise.
ISBN 0-8234-1711-5
[1. Monsters—Fiction. 2. Scientists—Fiction.
3. Music—Fiction. 4. Humorous stories.]
I. Kelley, True, ill. II. Title.
PZ7.E447 Haz 2003
[E]—dc21
2002017138

It is a dark and stormy night . . .

. . . but the lights are on at the Nutt laboratory.
Dr. Hazel Nutt is working late.
Dr. Nutt is a mad scientist.

"Of course I'm mad!" says Dr. Nutt.
"Igor ate my sandwich!"

Igor is weird, but sensitive.

Making monsters is Dr. Nutt's specialty. Just last week she crossed an Egyptian mummy with a fifty-pound candy bar.

"I really liked the Yummy Mummy," says Dr. Nutt.

"Too bad he melted."

"I feel like doing something special tonight," announces Dr. Nutt.
She goes to the supply cabinet and takes out a vampire head.

She attaches it to the body of an opera singer she has been saving for just such an occasion.

Will it work?

One bolt of lightning later and . . . yes!
It is the birth of Hazel Nutt's masterpiece:

Meanwhile, in Hamburg-with-Ketchup, the village near Dr. Nutt's laboratory, an important meeting is taking place.

"I have bad news," says Mayor Algernon Sense to the village elders. "Dr. Nutt is making monsters again."

"I still haven't recovered from the last one," shouts an older elder.

"You mean the Boogie-Woogie Man?" asks the mayor.

"Who else?" the elder replies, breaking into a strange dance.

"There is only one thing to do," says a younger elder. "Wake the villagers and storm Nutt's laboratory!"

Fifteen minutes later, all the villagers of Hamburg-with-Ketchup are rushing toward Dr. Nutt's lab.

"Why are we carrying these stupid torches?" the smallest villager asks. "Flashlights were invented years ago."

Back at the laboratory, Dracula-la-la is raising a fuss.
"It's lonely being a vampire opera singer," he complains.

Dr. Nutt gets an inspiration.

"Igor," she shouts. "Bring me that piano!"
Igor carries the piano over to Dr. Nutt.

"Now," continues Nutt. "Get me some of those spare monster parts."

A little stitch here,
a little electricity there,
and Dr. Nutt has created
the perfect companion
for Dracula-la-la.

The singing vampire and Frankensteinway are instant friends.

Dr. Nutt and Igor settle down to an evening of lovely monster music. But suddenly there is a pounding on the door of the lab.

"Arm Chair"
patent pending:
Hazel Nutt

Igor goes to the door.

"Concert schmoncert!" replies the mayor.

Then a lovely sound fills the laboratory.

The villagers are mesmerized by the beautiful music.

But Dracula-la-la is upset. "I'm not happy with my high notes," he says to Dr. Nutt.

"I think I have the solution," she replies.

"Perfect," says Frankensteinway.

Throughout the night the two monsters sing and play for the villagers. Dr. Nutt serves finger food. Igor sings backup.

The crowd's favorite number is "Old MacDonald Had a Bat."

Finally, after many encores, the concert comes to a close. Dracula-la-la and Frankensteinway promise to give another concert.

The crowd screams for Dr. Nutt.

"Dr. Nutt," says the older elder. "We'd like to thank you for such a wonderful evening."

"Thank you," says Hazel Nutt with a tear in her eye. "It's nice to be appreciated."

"And we promise we'll never storm your laboratory again," adds another.

To prove it, the mayor hands Dr. Nutt a key to the city.

"Shouldn't it be a key to the village?" asks the smallest villager.

It's that same troublemaker who wondered about the torches. There's one in every crowd.

"Walking-Stick" patent pending: Hazel Nutt

Dr. Hazel Nutt takes the key. "Thank you," she says again. "I know this will come in handy."